8 Ways to Make the Most of Storytime

FROM THE EDITORS OF
Parents.

1

BE AS DRAMATIC AS POSSIBLE.

It'll help the story stick in your child's memory. You could give a mouse a British accent, make a lion roar, or speak very slowly when you're reading a snail's dialogue. Have fun making sound effects for words like *boom*, *moo*, or *achoo*. Encourage your child to act out movements, slithering like a snake or leaping like a frog.

2

INVITE SPECIAL GUESTS.

Ask your kids if their favorite stuffed animal, action figure, or doll would like to listen too. Or curl up with the family pet. Including the whole gang will help hold their interest and make storytime seem more special. But if your child does start to lose interest before you've reached the last page, that's okay, because half a book here or a quarter of a book there still counts as reading!

3

KEEP LOVINGLY WORN BOOKS IN THE ROTATION.

There's a reason your kids ask for the same title again and again: a familiar story can be as comforting as a favorite blankie. The characters become their friends, and the books serve an important emotional purpose.

4

PLAY A GUESSING GAME.

When reading a new book, pause a few times to challenge your kids to predict what's going to happen next. Encourage them to refer to the title and illustrations for clues.

5

REFLECT ON THE STORY.

Talk about a book for a few minutes before you move on to another. Start a conversation with statements like "I'm wondering . . . ," "I wish I could ask the author . . . ," and "I'm getting the idea . . ." This helps develop your children's intuition and their ability to communicate a story back to you.

READ TOGETHER, BE TOGETHER is a nationwide movement developed by Penguin Random House in partnership with *Parents* magazine that celebrates the importance, and power, of the shared reading experience between an adult and a child. Reading aloud regularly to babies and young children is one of the most effective ways to foster early literacy and is a key factor responsible for building language and social skills. READ TOGETHER, BE TOGETHER offers parents the tips and tools to make family reading a regular and cherished activity.

6

CONNECT STORIES WITH WHAT'S HAPPENING IN REAL LIFE.

Suppose you read your child a story about a baby bird, and a day or two later, you spot a tiny sparrow in the park. Ask your child, "Doesn't that bird look like the one in the book we read yesterday? I wonder if it's looking for its mommy too?" Doing so will help promote information recall and build vocabulary.

7

CREATE AN IMPROVISED READING NOOK.

Storytime on the sofa or a cozy chair is sweet, but wouldn't your kids lose their mind if you set up a fort every now and then? It doesn't have to be fancy: just drape a blanket over two chairs, grab a couple of pillows, and squeeze in.

8

ALWAYS BE THE STORYTELLER AT BEDTIME.

You'll feel so proud when your little ones start recognizing and sounding out words on their own. But resist asking them to read to you at bedtime because it would replace this warm, wonderful bonding ritual with something that can feel like work for kids. Plus, they'll be able to listen to a more complicated book than they can read on their own.

llama llama misses mama

Anna Dewdney

VIKING

Llama Llama, warm in bed.
Wakey, wakey, sleepyhead!

Llama school begins **today!**
Time to learn and time to play!

Make the bed and
find some clothes.

Brush the teeth
and blow the nose.

Eat some breakfast.
Clean the plate.

Whoops!
Oh my—
we're running late!

Drive to school
and park the car.

Tell the teacher
who you are.

Meet new faces.
Hear new names.
See new places.
Watch new games.

Hang the coat
and say good-bye.

Llama Llama
feeling shy. . . .

Mama Llama goes away.
Llama Llama has to stay.

Strange new teacher.
Strange new toys.
Lots of kids
and lots of noise!

What would Llama like to do?
Llama Llama feels so new. . . .

Build a castle out of blocks?
Make a rocket from a box?
Llama Llama shakes his head.
Llama walks away instead.

Here's a little chugga-choo
with a captain and a crew.
Would the llama like a ride?
Llama Llama tries to hide.

Reading stories on the rug.
Kids are cuddled, sitting snug.

Would the llama like to look?

Llama Llama
hates that book.

Time for lunch! Now find a seat.

Llama doesn't want to eat.
Llama makes a little moan.
Llama Llama feels **alone.**

Llama misses Mama so. . . .

Why did Mama Llama **go?**

It's too much
for little Llama . . .

Llama Llama MISSES MAMA!

Don't be sad, new little llama!
It's OK to miss your mama.
But don't forget—
when day is through,

she will come **right back** to you.

Llama Llama, please don't fuss.
Have some fun and play with **us!**

Put on coats and run outside.
See the playhouse! Try the slide.

Tag and jump rope. Hide and seek.
Close your eyes and do not peek!

Now it's time to
draw and write.
Great big crayons.
Colors bright.

Take some paper
from the stack . . .

Teacher gets a good-bye hug.

Wave to friends on reading rug.

Climb the playhouse with the slide.
See if Mama fits inside.

Lots to show and lots to say!
Back again another day. . . .

Llama finds out something new—

He loves Mama . . .

and **SCHOOL**, too!

For Berol, my first to go off to school

VIKING
An imprint of Penguin Random House LLC, New York

Originally published as a jacketed hardcover in the United States of America by Viking,
a division of Penguin Young Readers Group, 2009.

Visit us online at penguinrandomhouse.com

Library of Congress Cataloging-in-Publication Data is available.
ISBN 9780593204948

Printed in the USA.

1   3   5   7   9   10   8   6   4   2

2020 Read Together, Be Together Edition